Aa Bb Cc

Ee Ff Gg Hh

Ii Jj Kk Ll

Mm Nn Oo

Pp Qq Rr Ss

Tt Uu Vv Ww

Xx Yy Zz

Alphapets

by Mandy Ross
illustrated by Neal Layton

introducing the sounds of the alphabet

Annie has an alligator in her attic

Aa

4

Bb

Ben has a buffalo in his bed.

Connie has a camel in her car.

Cc

Dd

Dan has a dinosaur on his desk.

7

Ellie has an elephant in her engine

Ee

8

Ff

fish food

fox food

Felix has a fox in his fish tank.

Gita has a gorilla in her garden.

Gg

Hh

Harry has a hamster in his hat.

Izzy has an insect in her ink.

Ii

Jack has a jellyfish in his jug.

13

Katie has a kangaroo in her kitchen

Kk

14

Ll

Lee has a lion on his lap.

15

Molly has a monster on her mat.

Mm

16

Nn

Ned has a newt in his net.

Ollie has an octopus in his office.

Penny has a penguin in her pack.

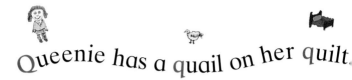

Queenie has a quail on her quilt.

Qq

20

Robbie has a rabbit in his rocket.

Sally has a seal on her seesaw.

Ss

Tom has a tiger in his tent.

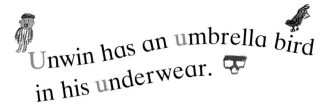

Unwin has an **u**mbrella bird in his **u**nderwear.

Uu

24

Vv

Vicky has a vulture in her van.

Wendy has a walrus in her wardrobe

Ww

26

Alex has an ox in his box.

Yousef has a yak on his yacht.

Yy

28

Zz

Zara has a zebra in her zoo.

phonics

Learn to read with Ladybird

phonics is one strand of Ladybird's **Learn to Read** range. It can be used alongside any other reading programme, and is an ideal way to support the reading work that your child is doing, or about to do, in school.

This chart will help you to pick the right book for your child from Ladybird's three main **Learn to Read** series.

Age	Stage	Phonics	Read with Ladybird	Read it yourself
4-5 years	Starter reader	Books 1-3	Books 1-3	Level 1
5-6 years	Developing reader	Books 2-9	Books 4-8	Level 2-3
6-7 years	Improving reader	Books 10-12	Books 9-16	Level 3-4
7-8 years	Confident reader		Books 17-20	Level 4

Ladybird has been a leading publisher of reading programmes for the last fifty years. **phonics** combines this experience with the latest research to provide a rapid route to reading success.

The fresh, quirky stories in Ladybird's twelve **phonics** storybooks are designed to help your child have fun learning the relationship between letters, or groups of letters, and the sounds they represent.

This is an important step towards independent reading – it will enable your child to tackle new words by 'sounding out' and blending their separate parts.

How phonics works

- The stories and rhymes introduce the most common spellings of over 40 key sounds, known as **phonemes**, in a step-by-step way.

- Rhyme and alliteration (the repetition of an initial sound) help to emphasise new sounds.

- Coloured type is used to highlight letter groups, to reinforce the link between spelling and sound:

and the King sang along.

- Bright, amusing illustrations provide helpful picture clues, and extra appeal.

How to use Book 1

This first book in the phonics series introduces the most common sound made by each letter of the alphabet, and the capital and small letter shapes.

- Have fun reading *Alphapets* aloud to your child (she* isn't expected to tackle the text herself at this stage). Emphasise the sounds made by the coloured letters.

- Talk about the sounds and pictures together. What sound can your child hear at the beginning of the words? What sound does her name begin with? What about her friends' names?

○ Phonic puzzles and games are great for learning. See if your child can think of another 'c' pet for Connie, or another 'p' place where Penny could keep her penguin.

○ Have fun together pairing up each of the children with their alphapet in the scene on pages 30/31.

Phonic fun

Playing 'I spy' games, or tackling tongue twisters together, are fun ways to practise letter sounds.

Help your child put together an alphabet scrapbook of things that begin with the same sound.

The text applies equally to girls and boys, but the child is referred to as 'she' throughout to avoid the use of the clumsy 'he/she'.